MY DAY WITH DOLPHINS

Gwen McCutcheon
Art by Jeremy Bennison

GRAPHIC READERS

Literacy Consultants
David Booth • Larry Swartz

Steck-Vaughn is a trademark of HMH Supplemental Publishers Inc. registered in the United States of America and/or other jurisdictions. All inquiries should be mailed to HMH Supplemental Publishers Inc., P.O. Box 27010, Austin, TX 78755.

Common Core State Standards © Copyright 2010. National Governors Association Center for Best Practices and Council of Chief State School Officers. All rights reserved. This product is not sponsored or endorsed by the Common Core State Standards Initiative of the National Governors Association Center for Best Practices and the Council of Chief State School Officers.

Rubicon www.rubiconpublishing.com

Editorial Director: Amy Land
Project Editor: Dawna McKinnon
Editor: Jessica Rose
Creative Director: Jennifer Drew
Art Director: Rebecca Buchanan

Printed in Singapore

ISBN: 978-1-77058-559-1
5 6 7 8 9 10 11 12 13 14   2016   25 24 23 22 21 20 19 18 17 16
4500568932

Will **Kim** take the **plunge** with **Missy** and **Marty?**

CHARACTERS

Missy and Marty

Shelly

Kim

Kim and her family visit an aquarium. They watch a dolphin show.

After the show, trainer Shelly asks the audience a question.

Would anyone like to be my assistant for the day?

To her delight, Kim is picked!

How about you, in the red shirt!

Kim is given a wet suit and taken backstage to meet the dolphins.

Welcome to the Marine Mammal Training Lab!

WOW!

Some people think trainers only teach dolphins tricks. In fact, we also take care of them, keeping them happy and healthy!

Kim commands Missy and Marty to jump through the hoops.

Jump!

How do they remember all this stuff?

So, do you think you're ready to get in the water?

Yes!

Dolphins are a lot like dogs. They're curious and playful, and they can remember simple commands.

While Shelly performs a trick, she surprises Kim with some exciting news.

Would you like to be my sidekick in this afternoon's show?

Really? That would be so cool!

Soon, it is time for the grand finale!

Last but not least, we'll show you how strong a dolphin can be!

First, it's Kim's turn...

This is amazing!

and then it's Shelly's turn.

YAY!!

CLAP!

CLAP!

After the show, Kim says good-bye to Shelly, Missy, and Marty.

Before you go, Missy and Marty have one more trick to show you!

Comprehension Strategy:
Identifying Main Idea/Theme

Common Core Reading Standards

Foundational Skills

3b. Know spelling-sound correspondences for additional common vowel teams.

Informational Text

2. Identify the main topic of a multiparagraph text

4. Determine the meaning of words and phrases in a text

6. Identify the main purpose of a text, including what the author wants to answer, explain, or describe.

8. Describe how reasons support specific points the author makes in the text

9. Compare and contrast the most important points presented by two texts on the same topic.

Reading Foundations

Word Study: Compound Words

High-Frequency Words: family, fish, happy, really, show, sound, start, teach, through, time, turn, water

Reading Vocabulary: assistant, dolphin, flippers, surface, swallow, teeth, trainer, trick, underwater, welcome

Fluency: Reading with Expression

BEFORE Reading

Prereading Strategy Making Connections

- Introduce the book by pointing to the cover and reading the title to the class.
- Have children make a text-to-world connection. Say: *This story takes place at an aquarium. Does this setting remind you of something?*

Introduce the Comprehension Strategy

- Point to the Identifying Main Idea/Theme visual on the inside front cover of this book. Say: *Today we will learn how to identify the main idea of a book by figuring out the most important idea. Books also contain important details that help explain the main idea.*
- Draw a concept web on the board. In the middle circle, write *There are many ways to help your community.* In the outer circles, write *volunteer at animal shelter, donate clothes,* and *pick up litter.* Ask children for more suggestions.

  Modeling Example Say: *As you read a book, try to figure out the most important idea. Our concept web shows a main idea surrounded by important details that support it. A book does not always say what its main idea is. Sometimes you have to figure it out using the important details. For instance, if the middle circle were blank, you could guess that the main idea is about how you can get involved in your community.*

- Say: *Good readers identify a book's main idea because it helps us understand what the author is trying to tell us. The main idea is the most important idea.*